IMPS, IMPS, AND MORE WIMPS!

IMPS, IMPS, AND MORE WIMPS!

CHARLOTTE M. PROSSER

ReadersMagnet, LLC

Imps, Imps, and More Wimps!
Copyright © 2020 by Charlotte M. Prosser

Published in the United States of America
ISBN Paperback: 978-1-951775-11-7
ISBN Hardback: 978-1-951775-12-4
ISBN eBook: 978-1-951775-13-1

All rights reserved. No part of this publication may be reproduced, stored in a retrieval system or transmitted in any way by any means, electronic, mechanical, photocopy, recording or otherwise without the prior permission of the author except as provided by USA copyright law.

The opinions expressed by the author are not necessarily those of ReadersMagnet, LLC.

ReadersMagnet, LLC
10620 Treena Street, Suite 380 | San Diego, California, 92131 USA
1.619.354.2643 | www.readersmagnet.com

Book design copyright © 2020 by ReadersMagnet, LLC. All rights reserved.
Cover design by Ericka Walker
Interior design by Shemaryl Evans

CHAPTER 1

I think this really started about a couple of years ago with a dream I had when we lived in a different house. I had this dream that this demon was trying to squeeze itself into my body, and when I woke up, I had my hand at my throat trying to choke myself. Nothing else ever happened until now. It was the last of June 1999, and I had this dream again, only I didn't let it take my hand up to my throat this time. When I dreamed that it was trying to squeeze into my body, I somehow woke up and I jumped out of bed and came to the dining room and fixed me a cup of coffee. I then stayed up. My husband got up after this and left for work. After a half day went by, I wasn't thinking about the dream anymore. This second night went by and I dreamed about me, my husband, Becky's mother and father had went out to eat. This dream was okay. So I had temporally forgotten about this other bad dream I had. I guess I had really pushed it to the back of my mind because a dream like that you just don't forget so easily.

Well, the next night, I had another bad dream. I dreamed that I was living in a trailer instead of this house I'm in and I was sitting at my kitchen table talking to my two daughter-in-laws (Becky and George's wife) when Becky's aunt walked in and she was holding a can of beer or a canned drink; we were drinking coffee, and she came in asking me for a cup of coffee, and I was so rude I told her she wasn't getting any of my coffee! I had a couch with no legs so it sits low to the ground, I told her to just sit down over on my couch and be quiet. I then found this worm in my floor and I poked at it with something, and about the third time I poked it, it turned into a snake. At the same time, this guy that was my ex-husband's brother-in-law came in and sat down beside Becky's aunt. I told all of them to hold their feet up because there was a snake in the house and it would bite. I remember him saying that he couldn't hold his feet up so it was just gonna have to bite him and then he would die. After he said this, the snake crawled up on my couch beside him and he reached out to pet this snake, and about the time he touched this thing, it turned into a white horse and galloped off. Then my dream ended. I was confused but upset about this dream. I knew it had some kind of meaning to it, I just didn't know what. I then started having feelings that someone was watching me or they were right behind me, following me everywhere I went. I could come up the hallway or come out of my bedroom, and it would feel like this thing was reaching out to get me. For the next couple of days, these feelings got stronger and stronger and it really got to where it really bothered me pretty bad. I called my mother and told her that I needed to talk to someone about these things going on in my house. And I don't mean a psychologist either, I mean a preacher! She called Phillip, a preacher at her church, and told him that I needed to speak with him alone at the church. They set everything up for me to speak with him at church at 12 o'clock Saturday, July 17, 1999. My mother and I went and talked to him about what was going on and told him about some things about my life, how I had been married before and what took place when I divorced my first husband. How he then married my sister. He prayed for me, and that day I got saved. Jesus was in my heart again! He also anointed my necklace that day.

When I left, I really felt a little better and I felt like all of my problems had been lifted away. The next day was Sunday and I went to church with my mother. I noticed that there was a small change around the house; it was like these imps decided to quit for a while. Around Wednesday, July 21, it had started up again. I could feel them watching me, following me, and reaching out to grab me from behind again. When Sunday came again, I decided not to go to church. My husband was at work and I was here alone again. I got my house cleaned up, except my bedroom, and my printer came on all by itself and sounded like it was printing something. It really scared me so I ran into my bedroom, grabbed a CD, and came back into the dining room. I then started playing "On the Wings of a Dove" over and over again. These little wimps didn't make this at all, so they really started up. George and his wife came down and stayed with me for a couple of hours and then they left and went to his brother's house because they were planning on moving in there with them. As soon as they left, the house started shaking like an earthquake was about to happen. I hung my phone up from talking to my mother and grabbed my keys, and out the door I went. I didn't bother to turn the lights off nor my TV, I didn't even bother to lock my front door! Nor put my shoes on. I went to Chris's trailer to get Becky, but she wasn't there. I did get George and his wife to come back with me. They spent the night, and after that, they just moved in with us. I think this is when I started staying up all night long, every night except when my husband was at home on the weekends. About Wednesday, things had gotten really bad as they were before. I guess I just got tired of this happening and I went to my mother's house and I told her what was going on and I got so nervous and upset, I went to crying. George had gotten a job at the mill, and one night when he left to go to work, he came flying back in crying, and he said that he had seen a demon sitting in the front seat of car. He didn't go to work that night.

Saturday came and I had dream #4. I dreamed that me, Becky, and George's wife was sitting at the table talking and my grandson (George's son) got hurt, he was in the living room. I told him to come here and my whole dream changed. The scenery was now that I was in bed and the devil was in the bed with me, trying to rape me. I pushed him away and yelled, "No," and then my dream ended. My daughter had called me two days before my birthday (my birthday is July 21) and told me not to get in touch with her again. She didn't want me to know her telephone number nor where she had moved to. I was told that she didn't want to have anything else to do with her family at all. After I had dream #4, I started seeing, smelling, and feeling these imps around my house. It smelt like someone had urinated on something, let it set for about two weeks, and then burned it! It smelt really bad! Anyway, I had gotten in touch with Phillip and he had come over and swept my house, and while he was doing this, you could really feel the heat from my bedroom. Al was standing in the dining room like Phillip told him to do while he and I went from room to room, and Al felt the heat so bad, his arms started sweating. After this took place, things were okay for a week, so this was the following Friday when I had dream #5. I dreamed that any oldest grandson (David) was getting on my bed with his coloring book and colors, and I was going to the bathroom. I left the door open and was telling him

David that he wasn't getting on the bed with his colors because he couldn't color on my bed; about the time I said that, Satan grabbed my shoulders with his hands and snatched me up into his face and said in a growling voice that he wanted me or he needed me or something to that nature, it startled me so bad my dream ended. I shot up out of bed, grabbed my housecoat, and flew out into the dining room. And to this day, I still can't stand for someone to talk to me in a growling voice. I will flinch every time, except when Philip does it. Saturday came, and I went to my mother's house telling her what I had dreamed. She called Phillip and anointed my grandson, and Phillip came to my mother's house and we talked about the dreams.

While was there, Phillip told me to put on the Whole Armour of God when this starts up again or really before it starts. I then left and came back home. Right after this dream is when my feet, ankles, and legs started swelling. We were still sitting up all night long. This dream really scared me because Satan was saying to me over and over, "This was not a dream, now you really are pregnant. See, how your feet are swelling, and your face is getting fatter too." And then he would laugh that irritating laugh! I was even getting sick to my stomach a lot too. One night, things really got bad! Me, Becky, Chris, and George's wife were sitting up, George had gotten him a job like I had said earlier, and he had just went to work when things started up. In George's bedroom, we saw shadows of my granddaughter's rocky horse rocking, things flying around, and some bed rails rattling that was under their bed. We could hear scratching in the walls, drawers in the bathroom slamming shut, whistling. They started playing with my hair, rubbing my legs and buttocks, and snapping their fingers in my ear. It upset me so bad, I went to crying. Becky and Chris called Phillip and he came over and set up with us from 11 p.m. to 4 a.m. While he was there, they kept playing with my hair and we had copied a picture on my copying machine and he was looking at it and found something evil on it. I don't know what he saw, but I saw the reaper on it, so I threw it away. That Friday, Phillip came over again and I was here with him by myself and we were talking about what happened, when I looked up and saw someone walk by my kitchen window, I kept waiting for someone to come through the front door but they never did. I guess had a puzzled look on my face about this, and Phillip said it was one of Satan's imps trying to find out what we were talking about. That spooked me! Anyway, the next day, Phillip, his mother, and his wife came over and blessed the house. They told me and my husband to sit at my table and hold on to each other's hands, so we did just like they told us to do. The night Phillip came over, he wrote down some things that he felt that night.

^CONFUSION
   DOUBT
^FEAR
   DECEPTION
   DESTRUCTION
   DEATH
   ANGER

He said that the two that had the ^ by them were the ones he felt the most that night.

After a week, little things started happening again that indicated to me that they were back. I also had dream #6, which was that Chris came to my house and had my daughter in the car with him. Chris said, "Look who has come home." She looked like she was so handicapped she couldn't even walk, let alone hold herself up. It was so real, I woke myself up crying. On top of all this, I had gotten a letter from her stating that we were not to get in touch with her at all, how sorry she thought her brothers were, and that she had to get away from me because she had gotten to close and she had gotten to where she wanted to be around me too much. I really got upset and called on Phillip's help once again. He met me at my mother's house and we talked. I showed him the letter that she had wrote to me and told him about dreams #4, 5, and 6. After we talked, I felt a little better. Things around the house were still going on strong.

Chapter 2

I once saw a shadow that looked like a man, standing in the vent of the air conditioner in the hall. August 10, my husband and I went to the Birmingham Airport to pick his niece up, and George and his wife had moved out and went to Phoenix City to stay with her mother. During this time and me talking to Phillip, I had found out that a member of the family has a demon inside of them. Phillip had warned me to watch this person very close, so I did and I still am; one day, I was in my closet in the bedroom after something and these imps scratched on the wall. It startled me, so I took my bottle of anointing oil and threw some oil up there. I was once was cleaning it out and, for some reason, looked through the crack of the door and saw one of them standing about middle ways in the floor on my husband's side of the bed. That is where they always hide. I came into the kitchen and got Becky and took her in there to see if she seen the same thing, she did! Al's niece looked and didn't want to see anything, George looked and saw it too. Chris said he wasn't going to look at nothing, he didn't want to see it, then one day, we heard some babies crying in my computer room.

That was the second night in a row that I had heard them crying, and it was the first night for them to have heard it. It is really a bedroom, but I once had the computer in there so I just call it my computer room. I went there to check out the noise we had heard, and a gush of wind came through me, and I twirled around and whatever had a hold of me made me lift my right leg up, and I was saying something weird and then about that time, somehow, I managed to say, "Jesus," and it turned me loose. I came out of there in a flash, and I was white as a ghost; two nights later, me, Becky, and Chris were up and heard the dryer going. I asked Becky what was she drying and she said she wasn't drying nothing like a dope. I went in there to check it out, and without thinking, I anointed it with oil before I rebuked it, and again, I felt a gush of wind and got twirled around again. The cabinet door slammed, scaring me like crazy. Chris was over there, and I thought he slammed it and I yelled at him, "Why did you do that for?" He said that he didn't do it, so I went and sit back down at the table so did Chris and he wouldn't go back over to the sink again either.

Before this had happened, Al's niece was sitting up with us, and she got startled when one of them snapped their fingers in her ear. After she got over that, she went to bed in the living room where we all went; when we got too sleepy, we couldn't sit up anymore. Then this thing happened with the dryer and we were sitting at a table when I started feeling sleepy, so we all went in there and went to sleep. Becky and I got back up about 4 a.m. the next morning, and we saw shadows in the living room. One of them looked they were jumping up and down in my recliner and then run across the floor and vanished. Then another one would do something, and it would looked like it would turn into a starry dust and go under my grandchildren's little recliner. I rebuked them and didn't nothing else happen for a little while. One day, Becky started badmouthing them and one of them snatched her hair. One day, I had my jewelry box out, and I decide that I would put it back in my closet, so I stated putting it up on the shelf and I also had a stuffed doll like the devil up there. That thing started moving behind my other jewelry box by itself and so I rebuked it and took it and threw it in the garbage.

The next day, Becky, Chris, George, George's wife, and Al's niece went to church and got saved. One morning, David came to me and said he wasn't going to sleep in my room ever again. His grandfather asked him why and he said that it was because he had seen a monster come out of my bathroom and go under my bed. We asked him what did this monster look like, and he said all he could tell us was that it was real hairy and had horns and it came out of my bathroom and went under my bed. A couple of days later, after I threw the doll away, I was going to check Al's niece's bedroom out because I had seen something go in there. This was not one of those wimps, this looked like stardust or something. I cracked the door open to ease my hand in there to turn on the light, but before I had a chance to turn it on, the light came on by itself, and I felt a hand rake across my hand. I snatched my hand out and slammed the door shut. We later eased the door open and turned off the light, but I anointed the room with oil first. September 29, Wednesday, around 11:15 p.m. 1 was woken up by something tickling me on my hands, in my ear, and then around my breast. I also heard noises in my closet sounding like they were slapping clothes racks.

Against each other and from side to side. The next morning when Becky and Al's niece got up, I found out that they also had heard some noises too. Al's niece heard them in the hall; it sounded like they were scratching the walls, and Becky heard sounds that sounded like they were knocking on the walls in the bathroom. The next night, I had two different dreams. One, I don't want to repeat, and the other one was about a bunch of angels and me were gathered around this white door and I could hear real heavy footsteps running toward us. Then the angels got startled about something, and they told me to come on I needed to hurry up. Before I went through the door, I woke up. I was really upset not about this dream but about the one I will not repeat. Before I had these two dreams about two weeks ago, I had started hearing real heavy footsteps running up and down the hall, and shadows coming to my bedroom door. I contacted Phillip again, and he came over, but I didn't get to talk to him because my husband was here and he did all the talking, and it sure wasn't about what I needed to talk to him about. However, I did get to talk a little and he anointed the house again. It still didn't work, because the very next morning, I got up real early and drink coffee until my husband got up and got ready for work. I saw something move around in Al's niece's room, and I went in there looking for it but found nothing. After my husband left for work, I looked in there and saw this real weird face looking back at me. I looked at this thing several times to make sure I was really seeing this thing; sure enough, it was. I then went and called Becky and asked her to look, but she didn't see what I was seeing.

October 4, Al and I went to church that night and AI got saved. October 5, 1999, around 5:05 a.m. I decided that I would go back to bed. I had gotten up at 2:02 a.m. because something had woken me up I was sitting in the dining room I started to hear some strange noises, like someone knocking on wall outside and opening the front door, so I decided that I would just go back to bed. When I got back to my bedroom, at the foot of my bed, I looked down the floor and I noticed a pair of orange cat eyes on the floor looking up at me. I also heard irritating laughter. I threw my housecoat at the foot of my bed and dove into the bed. As I was lying there, something touched my hips and was trying to pull me over to my husband and I wouldn't let it. I closed my eyes to say a silent prayer to God and something knocked on my nightstand beside my bed. I opened my eyes back up and they grabbed my hips and tried pulling me toward my husband again. When I wouldn't let it, it growled at me when it took my wooden cross and tried pulling it off of me, pulling it up in the air, I grabbed my cross and told the thing, "No!" I then started smelling some old spice shaving lotion and it got stronger and stronger like this thing had this stuff on him, and it was coming closer and closer toward me. When it got right in front of me, the smell disappeared, like this thing just vanished into thin air. My husband got up and got ready for work, and when he came into the dining room, I came too. Around 8 a.m., the kids started getting up and I told Becky what had happened. I had a plastic chest with two red handles on it, sitting beside my chair. I looked down at it and one of the handles popped open and started moving downward very slowly. I showed it to George and he was already looking at it, so I closed it up real quick and sit the chest somewhere else. Around 10:30 a.m., it got real dark outside and was really raining. George and Chris was gone and Al had gone to work because he had left at 6:30 a.m. to go to work. The only ones that were here were his niece and myself. She was in the tub taking a bath and I had decided to go back into my bedroom and get a pair of socks. When I opened the door, I had these wimps on my husband's side of the bed and under the bed. It sounded like they were playing with his cassette tape, which I thought was still over there in the floor. I found out later they weren't. I didn't take my eyes off of that corner of the room, but I slipped my hand in my sock drawer, got me a pair of socks, and backed out of my room and shut the door. I then heard someone shut a door down the hallway from my dining room where I was at. It was not my husband's niece because she was still in the tub and didn't come out of there for another ten to fifteen minutes later. I should have rebuked them, but I was so stunned till nothing like that even entered my mind. I contacted Phillip and finally got to talk to him about some things I wanted to talk to him about earlier. I also told him about what had happened this morning. After about an hour or two, he decided what we were going to do about this and I left and came home.

Chapter 3

The next morning, October 6, Al's niece got up and said that she had heard someone last night tapping on the window in her room, and beside a dresser, it sounded like someone was over there dropping stuff in the floor. I had gotten up real early again and I had heard car doors slamming, my dog barking like crazy, and it also sounded like someone opening the front door. Al's niece said that she also heard doors closing last night too, and she also had heard horns blowing. While we were talking about this, I heard her door open and I looked. I saw that it was cracked a little; someone was peeping through to see where we were. I called Al's niece's attention to it. I then got up to go back to my room and the computer room door opened a little and this strange feeling came over me, I stopped and came back to the dining room backing up to get my oil and went back down the hall. You could really feel them real good and even stronger in my bedroom. I oiled the hall and went back into my room oiling it as well. I later went to the bathroom in my room and heard something like water dripping in my tub. I wasn't sure what this was, so I rebuked it anyway and it stopped! One of these wimps started talking to me while I was in the bathroom. It started telling me that what Phillip had planned wasn't going to work, and I said, "Yes, it will," and then it said, "You don't even know that I am smarter than he is, so if you think he is so smart, what is he going to do, and when?" I said that I didn't know and because he hasn't really told me and that is when he growled at me again. I later came back to the dining room and was talking to Al's niece and the piece of paper that Phillip wrote down what he was feeling that night he stayed from 11 p.m. until 4 a.m. was lying on the table folded up, and the corner of it came up and back down like someone was trying to open it to read what he had wrote on it. These imps always talk to me a lot. You really have to watch them because they can really make you believe what they are saying is really true. They are so tricky too! They also can make you laugh. Like one day, I was getting a shower to get ready for church and one of them said to me, "That's right, hide behind Phillip's coat tail." And this last time it was saying to me, "Phillip, Phillip, Phillip, it's always Phillip, Phillip, Phillip, isn't it?" I really started laughing and my kids thought for sure I had flipped out completely. I couldn't stop laughing for at least ten minutes. I even went to my bedroom so I could try to get a hold of myself and quit laughing; when I finally did, it came back at me and said, "Don't laugh at me anymore and I mean it." I guess I had made it really mad, they don't like for you to laugh at them. Well, I started laughing again. This thing or these things have really put me through a lot of stuff. The day Phillip, his mother, and his wife came over to my house, I was here alone while my husband was gone to the store, and as soon as he left, they ran me out of my house. They have scared me so much until sometimes there, I thought I was going crazy. Sometimes I even thought that God didn't love me. They've even got me to thinking that I looked stupid, my family thought I was stupid and all kinds of different things. Lately, I have gotten to where I don't feel like I'm saved, although I know deep down that I am. But I also feel like Satan has woven a web or something over me to where I can't feel the power of Jesus. I can't even feel this in church anymore. When I do feel him and start crying, it's like the devil makes me stop. These emotions are hard to explain, but I did manage to explain them to Philip to where he could understand what I was trying to say.

My daughter had also called me that day, and about a month ago, my feet, legs, and ankles went down so they are not swollen anymore.

God does answer prays!

Chapter 4

Today is October 8 and it's 5:33 a.m. I have been up for a while and I went to go to this first bathroom, and about the time I went to touch the door, something slapped their hand on it. It sounded like they had a ring on their finger and the door did open up. After this happened, I just went to the bathroom in my bedroom. I had gotten up early, and as soon as I did, I could feel their presence, but it is really strong at the door of my first bathroom now. 4:15 p.m. I was at home by myself, but Al came in at 4:45 p.m. that's not but thirty minutes, but during this time, I saw a dim light flash down the hallway and heard voices down that way. I also felt the table shaking, and I was on the phone with Momma when I was picking with her. I said Phillip should be here in a little bit. I had already said that it was almost time for Al, but when I mentioned Phillip's name, I didn't hear anything else out of them. Then Al came in and I knew I was okay then, but before this, I even felt them again and I started to leave the house again. It's almost like they don't like me and they don't want me in this house. It's like they are jealous about something. There is something I really don't understand.

Ever since this has been going on, Al has never heard, felt, seen, or smelt them. Some of the things that go on around here is that you can hear something in another room that sounds like they are flipping the switch on the wall to turn the lights on or off. You can hear things that sound like the doors are opening or closing. You can hear car doors outside. Day or night, that sounds like they are right here in my front yard closing the car door. Sometimes, my fish tank sounds louder than usual. I mean the flow of the water, not the pump humming. Sometimes, things just get louder around here than they normally are. You can even hear them in my attic walking around sometimes. When these wimps are here, you can feel them because it gets extremely colder than usual. Since my feet, ankles, and legs have went down swelling, the tops of my feet are still very, very bruised and tender and it's been over a month ago since they went down. However, last night I was getting ready for bed, I noticed that they are beginning to swell again. When they were swollen the first time, I forgot to mention that they were two nights there that I woke up in a panicky mood. The first time was when my husband was at home and I woke up yelling, "Oh." My husband woke up also and he thought I was saying no but I wasn't. The second time was when we had started sleeping in the living room. I was in my recliner, and all of a sudden, I jumped up out of it and started yelling for my son (Chris) to help me. The reason was because I had gotten craps (charlie horses) in both of my legs. Once with my husband, I couldn't get awake enough to stand up for them to come out and the second time that was with my son was because I couldn't walk to get them out, I couldn't even stand on them. I still get them, but at least they are not as bad as they once were. Yesterday was Saturday, and about 10:30 a.m., we were taking my grandson (my daughter's oldest son) home and something tapped me on my left shoulder and on the elbow at the same time. I asked my grandson what

Imps, Imps, and More Wimps!

did he want and he said, "Me not want you, Nanny Prosser." I asked him didn't he tap me on my arm and he gave me a puzzled look and said no. I left it at that. That night, it was really weird though because I heard wolves howling so I thought it was on TV I later found out that Al's niece heard the same thing; she checked it out and found out that it was not on TV. Today is Sunday, October 10, and our revival starts today. I couldn't sleep good last night. I got woken up at 11 p.m. so I came in the dining room and started drinking a cup of coffee. I then went back to bed around 12 or 12:30 a.m. and tossed and turned for a while there. At 2:30 am. I was woken up again by David this time wanting to watch cartoons, then at 5 something, I got up. As I was sitting drinking coffee again, I heard a weird sound. I don't even know how to explain the sound. I looked in Al's niece's room without getting out of my chair because she had the door partly opened and it looked like the closet doors were breathing. As I am sitting here writing this down, I also heard something behind me playing with my what nots I have in my china cabinet behind me. I know what I heard in my china cabinet was real. Chris's daughter is now awake, it's 7:06 a.m. and she's the one that keeps saying that she is talking to the devil. Well, she sure was talking like crazy just now, but when I turned and looked, she quit talking immediately. It was just like the devil told her to quit talking because I was looking. I couldn't understand what she was saying, but I did make out two of the words, which was "bad" and "uh-huh." Like she liked whatever it told her, and she liked it a lot. She just got to talking again, but when I looked in there, she quit asking again. I know that there was no way she could have seen me neither time, but she quit talking like she had seen me. There was also a lot of growling going on in there, weird growling too. When I went into the bathroom, something hit the bathroom door very loudly, it sounded like they also was wearing a wedding band or some kind of ring when they hit the wooden part of the door. The door also came open a little. I just kept walking to my bathroom in my room. I also found out according to the evangelist that "these things I see and hear are not really happening." That's bull! I know what I hear, see, and feel is very real. I know I am not going crazy, and I can't make these things happen especially if the others are hearing it too! I am now all mixed up, but I know what is going on around here is real because Phillip says that the only time he has felt them was the night he sat up with us all night long. But he didn't say that he has or has not seen them or heard them. He hasn't said either way. I know he has seen them and felt them. He proved that when he swept my house and when he sat up with us. So I still have faith in Phillip.

Chapter 5

October 11 and 12 was okay, I just tossed and turned all night long. October 13, I didn't sleep to good at all. I kept having these real bad dreams and I kept talking in my sleep. I woke myself up a couple of times talking or yelling, "No, No, No, Don't." I just can't remember what these dreams were about. I do know though that they had something to do with demons. I also can still hear the light switches clicking like someone is turning them on or off. I just won't say anything to anyone because I now feel that they won't believe me anyway. Anyway, after all of this, I got out of bed after having nightmare after nightmare about demons and I also had this funny feeling. I came to the dining and sat down until everyone got up and then I went on my bedroom to get dressed, and for some strange reason, I got so nervous, I couldn't hold anything in my hands. I was the same way in the computer room, only it wasn't as bad in there. I came back to the dining room and drunk coffee until I got my nerves to settle back down. Later on, I was left here alone for a while, but everything was okay. October 14, I got up at 1:57 a.m. and came to the dining room and was drinking coffee. At 4:30 a.m., I had to go to the bathroom and I heard that sound again, like someone slapping the bathroom door with their hand and was wearing a ring of some kind, only this time it wasn't as loud as the one before. I can still feel them playing with my hair and necklace, every once in a while. I haven't told anyone, not after that evangelist said what he did. However, I do have to agree with him when he said that if I would play Christian music more, they wouldn't be here. I got up to get me some more coffee and looked down the hall and saw something into my computer room. I also still get this funny feeling like someone was looking in my window at my front door at me every time I went by. I just look and see nothing though.

October 15, Al and I had went to Mama's for a while after dinner and we went to the bookstore. We bought Mama a book and I bought a few things from Big Lots, which was next door. We dropped Mama off at her house and we came home. George was here alone, and when we pulled up, I looked in my living room window and saw a dark path of something in there. I really can't explain that and I don't know what you would call it. Its path was about five feet long, and it was a smoky gray in color. Al didn't see it. He just said that he didn't see anything and I was crazy. I didn't have any dreams last night, but I couldn't sleep because of my head hurting so bad.

Saturday, October 16, Al starts his rotation on his job today. He will now be working Saturday and Sunday from 7 a.m. to 7 p.m. and Monday and Tuesday from 3 p.m. to 11 p.m. and then he's off Wednesday, Thursday, and Friday. It was 3:30 p.m. eastern time, and George and I thought we had heard footsteps in the hallway. We ignored it, and as we were sitting at the table, when this piece of foil paper from a cigarette pack started rocking up and down like a seesaw.

This carried on for a while and then it was time to go get Al's niece from work, she got off at 7:45 p.m., but we didn't get home until about 8:30 p.m. eastern time. Al's niece was sitting at the table and I told her what happened with the paper foil, and just as I got it out of my mouth, it started up again. She put two more pieces down beside this one putting this one in the middle and the only one that would move was the one in the middle. We both laughed, and Al was at home at this time and he asked us what we were laughing about. We told him and he came in here to see, and it quit for about two minutes and then it started up again moving just a little. Al saw it and said that we were crazy and went back in the living room and sat own. It moved a little more then and I got my anointing oil out of my pocket and this piece of paper quit moving. I sit there with my oil in my hand for about three minutes before I put it back in my pocket; as soon as I did, this piece of paper started rocking again, slow at first and then it got faster. It was really weird because you could almost see the imprint of a finger on it. I can still hear these doors closing, but no one there to open or shut them, and sometimes I can see figures standing close by out of the corner of my eye. When I look fully at it, it's nothing there. It also still plays with my hair. Like it's doing now.

Chapter 6

October 17, I didn't have no dreams last night. It's now 3:55 a.m. and I guess I've been up for about fifteen or twenty minutes. George and Al's niece said that they would go to church with me today. I'm just sitting here drinking coffee. It is now 5 a.m. eastern time and I have decided to go lay back down. Al got up around 6:15 a.m. By this time, I was in a doze, but when he got up, it woke me completely. I told him he could turn the light on because I wasn't asleep, I was just lying there. He turned the light on and got ready for work and then turned the light back off and left the room. I just kept lying there and I started feeling something rubbing my leg and it felt like the mattress was shaking and bolting up in the middle of my bed. This really got my attention so I rebuked it and got myself out of bed. It won't be much longer before we get ready for church. We went to church, but for some reason, I was really depressed about something, I don't even know. When we got home, Al was already here and he said something about us going to church Sunday night, and I said that I really needed some more clothes because I didn't have anything to wear.

I don't remember what he said to me about that, but I told him that I have gotten to where I don't really care about going

IMPS, IMPS, AND MORE WIMPS!

anymore and he said that he wished I hadn't got him going if I wasn't going to stay with it. I feel that he should have talked to me about my feelings, instead of getting mad at me and blaming me for something I didn't do. I didn't make him go to church with me, all I did is ask him did he want to go. I can't make a fifty-year-old person do something they don't really want to do. Its 8:06 a.m., and I am sitting here asking God why did everyone think I was lying about what was going on here. Why would I lie about something like this? When just out of the blue, the cover I had on my birdcage came sliding off.

Phillip gave me a book to read and the name of the book is *Overcoming Anxiety and Fear*. Monday, October 18, didn't much happen except that it has gotten to where every time I go to my bedroom, I hear noises in there like they are trying to open me up in a corner for some reason. I went to my daughter's house and fell on her front porch. I really don't know how that happened. I hurt my leg and bruised it up, but it's not real bad. Tuesday, October 19, when I got out of bed, I had a bad feeling, but I ignored it lately, I've been getting those feelings every day. I took Al's niece to my daughter's house and came home. Little things are still happening here, but it's things that can be ignored most of the time. Wednesday, October 20, today is my daughter's birthday, but she didn't come down. We still hear doors closing in the house and cars doors closing outside. Sometimes you can even hear the motor of a car running, but no one out there. George walked over to sit down which was on the same side of the table that my China cabinet is on and my flower globe that he bought me started playing music, just out of the blue. Thursday, October 21, today I got up around 4:30 a.m. and I started hearing weird noises outside and sometimes it almost sounded like it was coming out of the computer room.

I also started smelling this bad smell, not like it was when this first started up, but a different smell. This smell was like burnt popcorn or something. It just felt of the side of my face as I was writing. Anyway I went back to bed about 6:08 a.m. and didn't get back up until 8 something. It hasn't bothered me until it rubbed my face a minute ago. They still keep playing with my necklace too. They've done this, the closing of the doors and all these little things so much till I've gotten used to it and it doesn't frighten me anymore. Friday, October 22, I got up around 1:45 a.m. I guess I had set in the dining room until 3:15 a.m. during this time, it kept sounding like something at my back door. That is why I went back to bed. While I was going down the hall, I really felt them all around me, I almost panicked. I got into my bedroom and it eased off some. As I laid in my bed, I could hear them in my closet again and I could smell something that smelt like clothes burning or was being scorched. I laid there for a few minutes so I decided to come back here in the kitchen. As I was coming up the half I felt their presence again. If was almost like they were gathering all around me, and it almost got me to running up the hall instead of walking. After I got in the dining room and got the lights turned back on, everything eased up. I just don't understand what is going on. Why are they after me so bad? I know the others hear them and feel them, but I'm the only one that has seen them in quite some time now. I know George saw one sitting in his car, and him and Becky saw that one through the crack of my closet door, but I think those are the only times they have really seen them. Just like now, I heard my table popping like leaning on it at the other end, my computer creaking like it is getting ready to come on, and this sound I hear over and over again. Before all of this started, I guess about four years now, I have felt a hand on my back. I

IMPS, IMPS, AND MORE WIMPS!

like to think that this is the hand of God or Jesus protecting me. This I can prove! I also have a picture of my house outside standing there dressed in a white suit. Becky says that it looks like someone on a horse, but I don't see a horse at all. I can now feel them in the kitchen when I go over there to fill my coffee cup up. Last night was the first night Al's niece stayed in her room for two nights. I can now hear something that sounds like two things made of metal clinging together. It will cling in my ear and then over to the bird cage and then stop for about five minutes and then start up again starting from the bird cage and going toward the front door. Then I heard a door creaking down the hall. I have also heard them a lot making noises in the wash room, so this means that today, they are all through the house. Like Thursday night, I was talking to Mama and I saw two of them jump from my computer and run down the hall.

Chapter 7

Today is October 23, and there's still nothing really bad happening. No more than usual anyway. They act like they have finally decided to give up, but that just might be what they want me to think. I am not going to let my shield down for one minute because I feel like it's just a trick. I wouldn't trust an imp anyway. I put all my trust in Jesus, and I feel that he will let me know when this thing is really over. Today is also George's wife's birthday and it is also the day Johnny died three or four years ago. I went to Mama's twice today, and once while I was there, the last time I went, my sister and my ex which is now her husband came in and when he me sitting there, he almost ran back into his car. My sister didn't really want to talk, but Mama told her I was talking to her, which I wasn't talking directly to her. I was talking to either one of them, her or Mama.

Sunday, October 24, today has been fairly good so far. I went to church and it was a pretty good service today, like always really. As soon as I came home, I started typing on the computer to catch up on this book, and it kept feeling like someone was walking up behind me. I could even see their shadow or what I thought was a shadow anyway, but no one was there, they were all in the living room, so I guess it was an imp beside me. They

Imps, Imps, and More Wimps!

really don't scare me that bad anymore though. I have hurt my collar bone somehow though. All day long, it has hurt me to move my arms in anyway. It even hurts to lift my coffee cup up with my right arm, and it's been like this since I got out of bed.

Monday, October 25, today nothing much has really happened. Late in the evening is when it really started up. Most of the time, it is late before it starts up. Anyway, it was around 7 p.m. and I was on the computer and I printed out some business cards of mine that I had fixed up, and on the back of them, I wrote a little verse called "Serenity" when these cards finished printing, one set of them kind of flipped up in the air like something was trying to turn them over. It kind of tickled me because I knew what was going on. About 8:30 p.m. George fed my fish and was looking down at the heater in the tank, asking me did it ever come on, about the time I said yes, something hit the side of the table where the tank is. We just looked at each other and went on about our business. My collar bone still hurts a little, I don't know what I did to it, but I have to keep taking Tylenol every four hours to kill the pain. Tuesday, October 26, today has been a very weird day. My collar bone is still hurting, my vacuum cleaner doesn't want to work for me, it is running okay, it's just hard to push it forward. It takes everything I have to get it to go. Things have been moving around and plundering with stuff, but I haven't really felt them as bad as I usually do. I also saw it raining outside my kitchen window, or at least that is what it looked like to me, but when I walked outside, it wasn't raining at all. George had went to his brother's house, but when he got back, he went outside to do something and he came back in saying that it was raining off of my house, nowhere else just off of my house. He saw it and felt it. It had gotten dark by this time, and Becky and Chris came over and was sitting at the table with us when the phone started turning around and an ashtray was on the table and it turned a little too. Wednesday, October 27, today is David's birthday, so we gave him his gifts and cake and ice cream, then George, Al's niece, Al, and myself went to church. I gave Phillip a copy of this book, what I had of it anyway, nothing happened here at the house. Except once, they started getting in my face (the imps) and patting me on my back like I was their best friend! I didn't have any more problems that night. Thursday, October 28, today is a different day. I heard them in my washroom and plundering all around the house, but they really haven't bothered me today. It was almost like they had decided to just leave. I thought that anyway, until the phone turned a half circle on the table. My collar bone has gotten some better, it hurts a little at the time now.

Anyway, we set up for a while and then we went to bed. Friday, October 29, today was really good. I never had a moment's problem out of them today. My ankles have been bothering me since Wednesday night. I went to Mama's for a while and talked to her about the way the people at the church has been doing and I had decided to quit going to that church and start going to another church, but I changed my mind again. Phillip has really been there for me when I needed him, day or night. I know that he is not the one that has gotten rid of these wimps, God did that, all by himself! But I felt really better just to know that Phillip was here with me. He knew what to do and what to look for, I sure didn't! He has also taught me a lot about the Bible and about these spirits. What I can do and just what I couldn't do. He said that I have really grown spiritually since all of this started. At first I couldn't see it, but now I can, I can really see it a lot now. One reason is because they can't scare me like they used to. They could scare me, but not like they could do at the beginning of all of this. Saturday, October 30, it was 3:15 a.m. and I was up at the table drinking coffee like I've done all this week. Everything was good and then I decided to go in the computer room to get a blue box to put this book in there and lock it up so nobody else could read it until I finished it. While I was walking down the hall, I got over George and his wife's picture and chills flew all over me, and then they did it again when I got into the computer room. After I came out of there, I could feel them behind me and beside me, coming up the hallway with me. I went over to get some more coffee and I felt them over there and in the wash room. I could hear this voice in my head saying, "Guess what, we are back!" I just said to myself, "Oh no!" I really don't think they went anywhere to be back. I went to my bedroom to get dressed, and like always, I felt them in there too. I kind of felt Iike they were going to get bad tonight because tonight is Halloween.

Chapter 8

Sunday, October 31, tonight was really Halloween, but they celebrated October 30 as Halloween. Phillip gave me a piece on this and it tells how Halloween got started and how you are celebrating the devil's day and his demons. I don't want no part of that mess! Anyway, George, Al's niece, Becky, Chris, myself, and the kids, David, Tiffani, and Chris's baby, went to church yesterday morning and just me, George, and Al's niece went last because I thought all of that was over with. Then last night, I had another bad dream. I dreamed that there were imps everywhere around me reaching out to grab me, it had gotten so bad, I yelled out in my sleep. This makes the second time I have dreamed this dream. Not the same thing happening, but almost the same. Some verses in the Bible that time I have dreamed this dream. Not the same thing happening, but almost the same. Some verses in the Bible that Momma or Phillip told me to read.

   2 Corinthians 10:3–9
   Ephesians 6:11
   Exodus 20:2
   James 5:15

Joshua 10:19
Mark 16:18
Matthew 5:17
Matthew 17:20
1 Peter 1:05
1 Peter 2:24
2 Peter 1:01
Revelation 7:15
Romans 8:31
2 Peter 1:01
Revelation 7:15

Tonight is Tuesday, November 2, and I'm sitting here at the table and I could hear talking coming out of the living room and I thought it was the TV going, but it wasn't on. It sounded like to a football game. No one was in the living room at all. After it had gotten darker outside, it sounded like someone getting up out of my recliner in the living room. George and I are the only ones here and both of us are in here in the dining room, so again, no one's in the living room. You could actually hear the foot rest on my recliner slam shut. George and I both heard that. I later told George that I wish Becky and Chris would come on if they were coming; just as I got it out of my mouth, the front door sounded like it had opened and then shut. It didn't because I have the front door locked. It is 8:51 p.m. and Chris and Becky still isn't here. I had also heard someone whistling at my birds earlier too. No one in the house was whistling, but I heard them as clear as day. I also heard them whistling with my bird. They are also tickling my neck on my right side real bad! It was beginning to make me mad! As I was writing this, I heard my front door knob turning like someone was trying to come in, but no one was there. Later, I heard my side door of my van slamming shut; however, no one was out there, so I just locked my doors with the remote. Chris and Becky shouldn't do me like this. Tell me that they will be here and not show up. Sometimes, I can't really tell about Chis, he has gotten to where he doesn't want to help me, none of his family. But he is always wanting us to him out and gets mad if we don't. But he will just about break his neck to do for Becky's mother, sister, and cousins. I just saw lights flash in my kitchen window would have been for a car to have pulled up in my yard. But they wasn't no one out there not even a car turning around.

I feel these little imps pretty bad tonight. I went to go to the bathroom, I heard them in the hall. It sounded like they were raking their hand up and down on the grate of the air conditioner and while I was in the bathroom I could hear a few of them groaning like they were really in a lot of pain. It's really bad too because it you just say out of the blue, "I rebuke you in the name of Jesus to leave this house." And you have company they would look at you like you was crazy. And then if you told them what you were doing, they would get up and leave your house and probably never come back.

It is now 10 p.m. and Becky finally showed up without Chris. As I was telling her, I saw them headlights in the window and said George saw them too. George said, "Well, I don't know about that now." Then Al finally came in and he read what I wrote down and laughed and said they have been in the living room a lot tonight then. Then we went to bed, and while my back was turned, he moves my foot step, scaring the wits out of me.

Wednesday, November 3, we went to church and Phillip and I talked quite a bit about my book, but he and Al also talked about my sign they are making me for my business. We were

IMPS, IMPS, AND MORE WIMPS!

rudely interrupted by some girl that use to go there. After church services was over, Al and I got a form to fill out to join the church. That morning, I was asking God to give me a sign if he wanted me to quit smoking and to give it to me in a way that I would know that it was him talking to me or however he was going to do it. Something said to me in a loud clear voice, "You'll stop smoking when I get ready for you to!" If I had been standing, it would have knocked me down in my chair. That night when we talked to Phillip about joining the church. He said that he knew I was smoking and not to let that bother me because they are not hard into that. So I feel that was God confirming what he said earlier, or at least now I feel that, that was him talking to me that morning.

Thursday, November 4, didn't much happen today. We went to Mama's late in the evening and she said that her knees had went down a lot and they have! We had requested pray for her Wednesday night and God answered our prayers. He has really been answering a lot of them for me though and has done a lot for me too! I will never, never, never forget how wonderful God is and has been for me. Friday, November 5, today has been a pretty good day. Some things happened but not much. I can go bathroom in my bedroom and flush the commode, and sometimes it sounds like something in it growling, and I heard something hit the front door, flush the commode, and sometimes it sounds like something in it growling, and I heard something hit the front door real hard around 5: 10 p.m. other than those two incidents nothing else has happened. Al and I changed the living room around. That is about all that has happened. But it's just 5:18 p.m.

Today is November 6, and like I said, last night was bad. Al and I went to bed about 8:30 p.m. After I got into bed, I could hear all kind of noises in here in the dining room and kitchen. The bathroom as well. This morning when I got up around 2 a.m. I came in and put some coffee on and started up the pot and I then went and sat down at the table got up around 2 a.m. I came in and put some coffee on and started up the pot and I then went and sat down at the table and I now have my birds in the living room and they started up real bad. Squawking and flapping their wings like they just had something to scare them pretty bad. When I turned the light on in there, they calmed down then. So I left the light burning. I came back in the dining room and was drinking coffee and I could really feel them around me. I heard them sometimes in my oven, and sometimes it sounded like they were in my washroom.

Today is Sunday, November 7, we all went to church and Sunday night. I didn't get to go because I had a bad case of a virus. I stayed at home and David stayed with me. He scared me more than the imps did. He was playing here one minute and gone the next. I would think that he was in the living room, and next thing I knew, he was running down the hall coming back in the dining room. I could hear the wimps everywhere, but I didn't rebuke them because the noises I was bearing I had l ready gotten used to. Monday, November 8, I heard these little wimps all day long rambling into stuff. We also found my clock in the computer room torn off the wall. I think that was the big boom I heard in there Sunday night. I went into my bedroom and I heard the bathroom door creaking open. I called for George to come in there, and when he came in here, I rebuked them and I slung my anointing over my door to the bathroom and it went all in floor. I didn't care as long as it got rid of them imps! George and I came into the dining room, and we didn't hear anything else out of them the rest of the night.

Tuesday, November 9. I really can't remember all happened Tuesday, so I guess I'll just say nothing happened as far as I remember and leave it at that.

Wednesday, November 10, Al and I went to see Phillip's job to get some letters they were supposed to do for me for my business sign but they weren't ready. He said that they would get them ready and he would have them at church when we came. Well, after we got to church, he said that they weren't ready or he forgot them or something. Anyway he didn't have them with him. I have tried three or four times to get these letters and about three times to find out how much they were going to charge me for them, they want give me a price and they won't do the letters, so I have decided to forget them completely. I think two weeks is long enough to wait for something like that, anyway, last night while we were at church, he told them that Al and I had decided to join the church and we stood in front of everybody and they all came up and welcomed us to the church. After this was over. He served preaching about Seven Acts of the Holy Spirit Text: 1 John 2:27, and he went to saying that verse John 16:14. This picture in the office fell, making a real loud boom! Everybody was shocked and didn't move a muscle. You should have seen the look on Phillip's face. He looked dead at me too! Finally, one of them spoke up and asked, "What was that?" They checked it out a few minutes later and found out that a picture fell off the wall. Me, Momma, and Al laughed the whole time this was going on. Then Al said, "Let Charlotte handle it, she's used to that."

Thursday, November 11. Today is Al's birthday. As the day winds down to an end, this morning I was sitting in a desk chair that we have, and all of a sudden, I heard something hiss at me, but it was in a real deep voice. Shortly after that, I had walked over to get me some coffee and a gust of wind came up into my face like it did when the things attacked me before. I ignored it but I almost didn't. I went back to the chair and the back of the chair kept flopping down like it was popping and it was making a loud noise. Then my daughter had went into my bedroom to get her son something to wear. They actually spent the night with us, but I think it was only because Al's niece was leaving for the next morning, and she was wanting to say good-bye to her. Anyway, she went in my bedroom, and after a few minutes, she came back in the dining room and asked me how could the phone ring in there when Al was still on the phone talking to his brother? The only thing I could tell her was to meet my imps. I don't think she really liked what I said and she acted as though she didn't believe me either, but the only thing I could do was to tell her the truth. After this was over with, it wasn't long before Al and I went to bed. My daughter's baby son followed us into the bedroom and slept with us that night. I think it really shocked all of us because my daughter said that he usually sleeps by himself.

Friday, November 12. It's now 2:14 a.m., and I've been up since 1:30 a.m. and Al's niece goes to Virginia today, so she can get home for Christmas. Al said that we need to leave here around 5 a.m., but we left at 4:30 a.m., and after we got there, we had to wait for almost an hour before she hoarded her plane. We left and took my daughter and her two boys home and then we came home. We hung around the house and Al finished my sign for my business and got it up. We really didn't do much of anything else after that. I have noticed that for the past two weeks, I haven't heard the switches flip on or off in the other bedrooms.

Saturday, November 13, today was a good day, it really got hot outside so Al put the Christmas lights up and decorations for outside. He said that he was gonna go ahead and do this while it was pretty outside. George was here and Al made him help, but I don't think he was really wanting to. He acted like he really didn't want to do anything. He even asked why Al was putting them up so early, and then he said he was going to eat something first because he felt weak. I know that he misses his kids, but he won't do anything about getting visitation right so he can see the kids. If I mention for him to do something, he gets mad, so I've decided to let go of it and let him do what he wants to do.

Sunday, November 14, George went to Chris and Becky's last night. I thought he would be here in time to go to church but he wasn't. Al and I left here around 10:15 a.m. going to church and we never saw George. I still haven't heard from that guy I wrote about getting my book published and it's been a while now so I guess I'll have to find somewhere else to write about it.

Chapter 9

Monday, November 16, a lot has happened today but not so much with these imps, Al and I had the biggest argument. He got up ready to start fussing at George. He's always fussing with one of my kids about something. I get so tired of it till this time when he started up on him, I exploded! He told me that I wasn't nothing but a big burden to him and have been for quite some time. That really hurt my feelings a lot and I don't think I will get over it none too soon either. I know I said a lot of ugly words and I asked God to forgive me for sinning too! I know he did, but I still want to go to the altar. Wednesday night when I go to church, I feel like I need to this time. After about two hours, he finally came back in the living room with me, but I will never feel like I'm a part of his family again.

Tuesday, November 16, today Al starts a new shift at work. Now he will work from 11 p.m. to 7 a.m. Monday through Friday, except for Wednesday he works 7 p.m. to 7 a.m. and is off on the weekends. Last night, I didn't sleep in my bedroom because Al wasn't here, so me, George, Becky, and Chris sit up. Chris went to sleep pretty early, and then it started up, not bad but it still start up. First, Chris and George went to the store and Al left before they got back, leaving me and Becky there by ourselves and I started seeing something that looked like a reflection in the water, but this was on the ceiling. I showed it to Becky and she moved because it was right on top of her at the table. We watched that for a long time, and I even rebuked it but it didn't do any good. Then Becky saw a shadow down the hall that looked like someone was standing there with their hands on their hip. I also tried to get something out of the freezer and these imps kept trying to close the lid on my hand. The lid would come down a good ways and then back up again. They also started feeling of the left side of my buttocks again and I was over at the stove and they tried to do something to me over there too! We sat up until 1:30 a.m. or around 2 o' clock, and we went in the living room to go to sleep. I really couldn't go to sleep, so I just laid there in my recliner until I dropped off to sleep. Around 3:30 a.m. and 4 a.m., things started up again. I heard them in the attic off and on until I got up at 5:30 a.m. They sounded like they were walking everywhere up there and then once it sounded like one of them were running and they tripped and fell over something. I could even hear them talking pretty loud in the hallway too. I think that is when I got up. I don't know what is going on! Phillip said once that this could be caused from some of my in-laws talking bad against me. I was talking to a sister-in-law back when I gave Phillip the book to read, and I told her what he had said, and she said, "I guess I need to start good things about you then, so these things will go away." While I was sitting here typing this into the computer, I heard something under my desk that holds my printer and then my printer came on by itself. So I guess this stuff is going to start up again, just because Al won't be here. Well, I think I'm ready for them this time!

Wednesday, November 17, we all went to church and I told Phillip what had happened and told that I wanted to get rededicated tonight and he said he would do it, but he never did, so I left and came home. Phillip has a bad habit of saying that he will do something and then doesn't do it. Thursday, November 18, didn't anything happen tonight, but I think it was because I had been talking about the Bible and I also had been reading the Bible some too. We all went to bed pretty early that night, and like always, I got up pretty early. I found my son's daughter in some of my beads and she had poured them out in the floor and she had gotten into another one of my boxes that had my canvas in it and had that stuff all over the floor. We got pretty upset with her and she was gotten on to and then we left to take Chris to court on a matter that they had wrongfully accused him of. They postponed it until December 16, so he could get a lawyer to defend him.

Friday, November 19, I was sitting at my dining room table and I saw a starry dust thing go into my first bedroom through the crack of the door at the top this time instead of the bottom or side of the door. I didn't say anything to anybody, I just kept my mouth shut. After this I was talking to my mother on the phone and when I said something about George's wife, the table just shook like crazy. Like a dope, I look under the table and about that time it dawned on me that something might be down there, but it wasn't. About thirty minutes after this happened, Chris and his family came in. I sent my two boys to the store to get us some cigarettes and my husband had left to go to work and me and Becky was here by ourselves. We started hearing these imps everywhere, and it seemed that they were everywhere! We saw one standing in the hall with their hand propped on their hip, I saw a shadow in there moving back and forth, and they looked as though they were going in and out of my room over and over again. I thought that it was gonna get really bad that night, but it didn't. Once I saw one standing beside me out of the corner of my, eye and when I looked, it acted like it was going to slap me in my face, only it didn't make the connection. Came pretty close, but it still didn't do it. It made me flinch though. It had also made me mad so I took my oil and threw some over that way, nothing happened. We heard them growling a lot too, but I couldn't figure out where it was coming from.

Saturday, November 20, George went to Phoenix City to talk to his wife, and Al and I stayed at home. When they finally came in, his son and two daughters were really excited about being there. They said that my youngest granddaughter will be wearing glasses about six months from now. They said that his son won't eat or drink anything, he won't even tell her when he has to go to the bathroom. So last night when he came in, he started eating, and this time, he was chewing everything up like he was supposed to and he was talking to me like crazy!

I think it is just he's glad to be home and he showed it. The oldest girl came right on in, and the first thing she said was that she had her cast off. They were really excited to be here, but they took them to my younger son's trailer. Tuesday, November 23, some days have went by without anything happening, so today as I was sitting here, I got to thinking about what all that has been happening. I got to talking to George's wife and we got to talking about stuff that had been happening over in the blue house and we gotta compare what I remembered and what she had remembered and I think we hit it right on the nail head because these imps started up and they wouldn't let up none too easy either.

Over in the blue house, the night before I dreamed that bad dream, I had a dream were some people were trying to get in my house. They were banging the door with their fists, yelling,

"Let us in, please help us, let us in." That next night is when I dreamed that that imp was trying to squeeze itself into my body, and when I woke up, I was trying to choke my own self. After I had this dream is when things started getting weird around there. We couldn't go to the bathroom without having the feeling that somebody was watching us. The grandkids' toys that played music would start up without it being turned on. I couldn't even go outside without it feeling like someone was out there watching me too. This is also when George's wife saw someone or something sitting on the headboard of her bed looking down at her and was watching her sleep. She had also felt something or someone rubbing her hand. We didn't live there long after that, but it wasn't a short time either. It was something like a year and something and then we moved into this house and for a while it was okay. But now it isn't.

The way things started around here is first, my husband said that he thinks that we have rats because they sure were playing a football game in the attic one night. I told him no, we did not that he was just hearing things. Two mornings later, I heard the same thing up in the attic. We had already moved everything out of the attic so I knew that there were no rats up there now. Then one night, I was picking at Chris's wife over the phone and told her that my straw was turning around in my glass like I was stirring something up, and I was making it do it because I had powers. Then I told her that it wasn't funny anymore because some of my drink had just disappeared out of my glass. Shortly after this night is when I had that dream, only I didn't try choking myself. Tonight as I write this down, I can feel them all over me.

Chapter 10

I saw something on my bed, but when I reached for it, it disappeared. George's wife saw it and she saw it vanish too. After this happened, my foot stool starting vibrating like crazy. I left out of there and came back to the dining room. I still feel them imps pretty bad, and when I got back into the dining room, I felt the floor in there vibrate and it is a cement floor. I could feel them all over my body and they were playing with my necklace and I later could see them standing all around me. This time, I called my husband at work and told him what was going on. He couldn't get off work at that time because he was having problems himself at work. As I started writing it all down, I had a receipt on the table from Walmart, and it flew about a foot in the air and came back down landing over my keys. Then I started seeing them all around me again. I also saw them in my hallway tonight, too. It even looked like they were going through my walls too. It's been over an hour and my husband was going to call me back he hasn't called me back yet. So now I'm just sitting here waiting for his call and wondering what was going to happen next. After George complained all night long about sitting up, he said that the doctor told him that it wasn't good for him to sit all that long. He was talking about an injury that he had just had for his back, about two years ago. He complained all night long until I got mad and told him that we would go to bed. He also started pacing the floor and dozing off. We went to the living room and he was asleep in no time, so now I'm up by myself. I got into my recliner and I kept hearing the imps in my dining room and I heard the dishwasher going without anyone starting it up. I guess I had dozed off myself because my husband came in around 5:05 a.m. and we went to bed. Al was having a hard time at work and he got wrote up for leaving.

Wednesday, November 24, today started off as a kind a weird day. I still can feel the imps around me, only they followed me up town and outside of my home. Everywhere I went I could feel these little wimps! Around 6 p.m., I called Phillip at church and talked to him for a few minutes and told him what happened. He spoke to Al and then they hung up. He talked to me about what he had said before, about the problems that was lingering these things around here are still problems that haven't been solved. He just didn't tell me what these problems were so I could get rid of them. He did tell Al that we needed to pray like we did before both of us together and pray for the blood of Jesus to cover us. So before Al went to work, we did just that. He also told Al that they would pray for us in church too. The night is just about over with and I heard them in the bathroom once saying, "Psst… psst," and then I saw them once in the hallway flying over or around the light, and I felt water drip from the ceiling on to my hand. Which wasn't no way the air could've caused that because of the way it is made. Other than that, it has been a really good night.

Thursday, November 25, Friday, November 26, Saturday, November 27, and Sunday November 28, were pretty good. My husband was here all four nights, and I got a pretty good rest out of it too. We went to church Sunday and I talked to Phillip about all of these things that were happening again and he gave me a hook to read and that has scriptures from the Bible to read and that will help me deal with these things.

Monday, November 29. We sit up again and nothing happened too much. Tuesday, November 30, didn't much happen. If it did, I have forgotten about it from being so tired. Wednesday, December 1, tonight we should have went to church though because they were celebrating Phillip's birthday after church tonight. Thursday, December 2. I started feeling these imps around me again, taking every step I took, every turn I turned. I could see lights flashing like someone was turning around in my driveway, but no one was there. I have noticed one thing has stopped and that is the clicking sound you hear someone turns the lights on or off. I haven't heard that in it while now, about 21/22 weeks now. Tomorrow is Saturday, December 4. We had a pretty good day today, although Thursday night I had a bad dream about some kind of iguana or oversized lizard attacked me. I finally killed it I guess because it disappeared and I woke up. But Saturday, December 5, we went to church, meaning Al and I. We went Sunday morning and Sunday night and things around here were okay. Phillip gave me two Christian music tapes and I guess that is why it was okay. I haven't listened to neither. I also had a really good, good night sleep. I think I sleep from Friday evening to Sunday morning and then off and on Sunday.

Monday, December 6, not too much has happened today, I have felt them but not nothing, like it usually is around here. I was also pretty busy today too. I went into my room for things in my closet last Monday night and I heard them making all kind of ruckus in the bathroom so I scooted on out and I can still see them from the corner of my eye. Tuesday, December 7, Today was a good day, I thought I was going to have a lot of problems with them, but it turned out that everything calmed itself down.

Wednesday, December 8. Al went to work from 7 a.m. to 7 p.m. today so until then everything was okay. I started having problems with them in the hallway, but when I said something about playing those tapes that Phillip gave me, everything calmed down. We went to bed kind of early and I slept until 5 off and on then I got on up.

Thursday, December 9, today has been a really good day. I have been real busy again today but so far it has been a good day.

Friday, December 10, today I had a good except Al came from work and something grabbed his leg which he said that it was one of my grandchildren, but it wasn't, she was on the other side of the room.

Sunday, December 19, today was a good day. I have missed a lot of writing in this book, so I will just tell what I can remember the other days that I have missed. I do know that Al is beginning to hear these things around here, but he is still in denial right now. He has heard them knocking on the door when there was no one except us around. I heard them doing a lot of stuff, but it is just little things that can ignore. One day I was sitting the table and they started moving paper around again, and they are still playing with my necklace. They keep trying to take in necklace off a lot for some reason.

Today is January 7, and it is Friday. On January 4, 2000, which was on a Tuesday, I had another had dream. I had asked God to help me through this situation with Chris and Becky because they have changed and this time for the worst. They are letting some of her family live in with them and I have been told by a lot or people, including her family, that they do drugs really bad. I don't like for these people to be in the trailer with them and I am planning now to kick these people out. Anyway, after me praying tor some guidance from God and me tossing and turning for about an hour, I went back to sleep and I dreamed that I had went to Chris and told him that I wasn't going to these people stay there anymore and they were making too many bills for his check. He as usual got mad at me and mumbled something. I couldn't understand what he had said, but I know it had something to do his SSI check and me being his representative or it. We then got in a car that he had and they were supposed to be taking me home, but instead we went to Becky's mother's house. I got out with them to talk to Becky's mother's house. I got out with them to talk to Becky's mother. But this woman posing as her mother wasn't Becky's mother. I talked to her for a while and it sounded like she was Becky's mother but she didn't look like her mother. I finally asked her where Becky and Chris went, and she said that they went in her sister's room to see if they could borrow some money but her sister was at work and then this woman laughed. Then it dawned on me that if Becky's daddy and sister was at work, so was her mama. I went into the living room and waited for Chris and Becky to come back. I guess in my dream it was about an hour or two and when they came back in we left, but this time I was driving my van. I had went about three blocks down the road, and Becky said that I was going to have park my van and go through this building that looked like some kind of mall so I could get over to the other side. While going through the this mall, I had to go to the bathroom; the first one I came to wasn't nothing but shower stalls, and when I opened door, the first thing I saw was oldest son's boy standing there, looking puzzled. I looked around to see what he was looking at and I saw his mother drying off. I looked at another stall and another woman was getting dressed. I left out or there and found that I thought to be the bathroom, and all of a sudden, this black junkie came in there and pulled a switch blade on me. I looked shocked and just out of the blue, my oldest son, George, popped into the picture and he handed me a knife like that one too. This black man started swinging it at me like he was going to try and cut me so I did the same, only I did cut him on the first joint on his ring finger, down where his ring met the joint of his finger. I looked at George and he was gone, and when I looked back at this junkie, he was gone and the dream ended. I never did find Chris and Becky again. January 5 and 6, I can still feel these imps around but they have calmed down a lot. I do hear them once in a while, sounding like they are leaning on something. You can hear things squeaking and a lot of other stuff that is really hard to explain, I just know that they are still here. Sometimes I can see them still out of the corner of my eye.

Chapter 11

Saturday, January 8, 2000. I have felt them hanging around here like they are waiting on something. What, I don't know. They have been making a few sounds just to let me know that they are still here. Sometimes it is easy to ignore them but sometimes not! I also had a couple of more dreams that night before I woke up. One of them was a bad dream. It was really but both of them was really. The bad dream was of one scenery, which was what looked like a spine from someone's back in a puddle of blood, but this spine was moving or crawling, whichever way you would what to say it. And the second dream was, I saw this beautiful bright star and it kept getting bigger and brighter, and after it got just so big, I see Jesus's face, and then that dream ended. Sunday, January 9, today has been a fairly good day. I haven't heard much from them today at all.

Monday, January 10, today has been a really rough day. I got up at 2 a.m. and they were really bad then. They were making noises a lot. You could hear them walking in just about every room in the house. They would rattle stuff, like paper, etc. just to aggravate me. Yesterday, they would look out of my computer room, close the door, and then look out of it again and it is getting unnerving, but I have prayed to God again and it is getting better. They even moved my belt on the kitchen table this morning. Tuesday, January 11, today started off about the same way it did yesterday. Only around 5:32 a.m. I was in the bathroom and it sounded like someone called to the bathroom door and stopped. I thought it was Al, but I found out later that it wasn't. That was a little spooky for me, but now I have my Gospel music on so maybe everything will be okay.

Wednesday, January 12, today has been a bad day. I started off with me going to the bathroom around 5:32 a.m. and I had left the door cracked a little, but not to where anyone could see in there. I heard someone come up to the door and stop. They just stood there for a while, and when I flushed the commode, I could hear them going back down the hallway. When I came out (I thought it was Al), I went to the hallway to my bedroom to see if Al was up but he was still sound asleep, then is when I knew for sure what it was. Alter Al went to work, he called me, I asked him did he come to the bedroom door and just stand there and he said no, he didn't. He said he didn't have a good night didn't either; he didn't know what was going on, he just couldn't sleep. I put on my Gospel music again until the kids got here, and everything was okay. Juanita came down and Chris and Becky took her back home, George, his wife and kids, and myself got ready for church. But before then, I had been talking to Mama and I told her about what was going on and that I might get Phillip to come and sweep the house out again. I just didn't know if it would work again or not. While I was getting ready for church though, the telephone line beside my bed went to moving and I couldn't do anything because my foot was in my pant leg and I couldn't get it through as fast as I wanted to. I went to church and talked to Phillip about what was going on. I really don't know why I keep bothering him about what is going on because he can't really help what's going on, all he would be able to do is pray about it, and I can do that myself. I think Phillip has a lot on his mind and then when I think about it, it makes me feel bad for imposing myself on him and depending on him like I do when these imps wants to cut up like they do. I guess that has become a source for me and one source I'm gonna have to get out of. I also requested prayer for Mama because she wasn't feeling too good that night, but he forgot until his Mama reminded him of it. The way he keeps forgetting to request prayer for me or Mama is why I feel that he must have a lot on his mind. Especially when it hasn't even been but about ten to fifteen minutes since I've said something about it. I just know he doesn't do it on purpose. I really can't remember if anything happened Wednesday, Thursday, Friday, and Saturday or not, but Sunday, Al and I went to church and I really felt close to God. Closer than I ever felt in a while. Nothing happened at the house except they still keep the water cold when I take a shower. That's been going on for almost a month now. Sunday night, Al and I went to church and we took Juanita, John, John Jr., and Joshua with us. They really had a fit over Joshua. I didn't feel Jesus so close to me like I did that morning, but it was close.

Monday, January 17, I got up at 2:44 a.m. and I sat up until 4:30 a.m. and I then got back up when Al got up to go to work, around 6:00 a.m. I got up and came to the dining room and poured me a cup of coffee and sit at the table to drink it and I told Al that I was cold so he told me to turn the heat up. I turned it up and it sounded like someone in the bathroom (which was right behind me) and they slammed the toilet lid closed. I turned to look because the door was standing open but I didn't see anything. I then knew that it was them imps again.

When Al left to go to work, I put on some Gospel music. It isn't playing now though and I have heard a few noises but not many.

Tuesday, January 18, didn't much happen, however, I did hear their presents around the house. Wednesday, January 19, today is another day. I have heard them since I got out of bed. While I was at the computer, I could hear something that sounded like they were growling at me, and it also sounded like I had disturbed them once when reached under my desk and pulled my paper cutter out from under it. They had made a really weird sound, I can't explain how it did sound, unless I explain it like it was a pack of wild dogs growling with food in their mouths. Later, I went to the bathroom and I noticed a shadow on the wall beside my towel and I thought, *Well, that is a really weird shape.* I came in the dining room and got a sheet of paper and hunted up a pencil and went back in the bathroom and traced this shadow. When my two daughter-in-laws came over, I took them in the bathroom to show it to them, and the shadow was gone! I then realized that, that wasn't the shadow of my towel, it was one of them!

Then that stirred me up a little. Thursday was okay and Friday, January 21, I had just a little bit of commotion going on and my grandson, David, was here and he asked me was that those "monsters" I told him that I don't know, but I think so. That is when he asked me did it look like that ghost that was behind me. I snatched around and there wasn't nothing there. I told him not to be doing that anymore.

Saturday, January 22, didn't nothing happen because Al was at home. Sunday, January 23, at first nothing happened. Al slept late, so I wasn't able to take a shower for church. I guess I could have but I didn't want to take a chance of waking him up. Anyway, when he got up, he kinda got mad at me for not getting ready for church, he got dressed and went without me. As I was sitting there at the dining room table, I was reading my book, checking it for mistakes when a receipt I had lying on the table turned a half round on the table without anybody touching it, there was no air stirring either. Well, that kind of motion got my attention quick! I quit reading long enough to put my Gospel music on my stereo, and I turned it up so it could be heard in every room of the house.

Today is Monday, January 24, I got up at 5:18 a.m. and around 5:45 a.m. as I sitting at my table, I heard this tune, one tune, behind me, so I turned back facing the table, and I heard it again. I found a little Oscar car that belongs to my baby granddaughter and I then that it was that. I told these "imps" that, that was enough, I didn't want to hear any more of it, and I then turned back facing the table again. When I turned back to the table, it decided to play three notes and then four. I took my oil out of my pocket and put some on and told them again that I said that, that is enough. One more note came out so I rebuked it then another came out and then it didn't play anymore until after Al got up, got dressed, and was sitting at the table drinking coffee with me. I said, that is enough! It is now 9:08 a.m. and I haven't heard any more notes coming from that little car.

January 25, Tuesday, didn't much happen today. I started feeling a little weak because of this virus that has been going around. I think I got it.

Wednesday, January 26, today nothing from the imps, I was going to go to church tonight, but George said he couldn't go because the kids didn't have anything to wear, so I decided not to go and then the next thing I knew he was saying that he was going to go. I told him that I had already decided not to go now! So none of us went to church.

Chapter 12

Thursday, January 27, I have felt them a little today, but it hasn't been too bad at all. They still do just little things to let me know that they are still around. It's still confusing to me. I don't understand why they are still around. What do they want? I know that it could be a lot worse than it has been around here. I really don't understand what is going on.

Friday, January 28, today has been okay, Al and I and got our taxes done after he got off work. I usually do them, but I just didn't feel like doing them this year. We went rapid refund which was supposed to be back in two to four days but haven't gotten them back yet. I still see shadows here and there every once in a while. Hear them in my what nots or in one of the rooms. But nothing like it was back in July. I can still feel them around me, feel them playing with necklace, or whistling in my ear. They haven't snapped their fingers in my ears for a long time now and I sure am glad of that.

Saturday, January 29, today was a good day. Al was at home and nothing happened. Sunday, January 30, today is a good day it is cold and raining. Al, David, my grandson, and I went to church this morning. After church, I really got to feeling sick. I felt like I was very weak. I was coughing like crazy and couldn't stop. I guess I had a virus. It was such a good day. I did all of my washing and I cleaned my bedroom up real good. I changed the sheets on my bed, cleaned my drawers out. Then I cleaned my husband's drawers out, and then I did David's. All I had to do on mine was my socks, nightgowns, and shirts. Same with the others though. I even vacuumed the room out. Dusted the furniture and everything else.

Tuesday, February 1, I had a lot of running around to do today, but when I got home I was feeling a lot of discomfort in my bedroom. I ignored it and acted like there wasn't anything there. After a while, it went away. I hope everyone understands that in order for this to be, I have done a lot of praying to God. For these things that is so evil to leave my house. God has answered my prayers. That's I haven't been having all that much trouble with these little imps anymore. Every once in a while, something will happen and I will pray to God again, and he removes them. I'm so glad I have the power of God on my side!

Wednesday, February 2, today has been a good day too. But I stayed pretty busy. George and his family moved back in with us and he started a new job today. I had some bills to pay and Juanita and the kids came down and she went with me to pay them. After she left, me, George, and his family went to get some groceries. I came home and cooked dinner while putting groceries up. I burnt some of the fries and the pork and beans in the process of trying to do too many things at one time. We didn't go to church tonight either. I didn't feel too hot and I don't think Al felt too good either. He is fixing to change shifts again and he didn't have to work from 7 a.m. to 7 p.m. today. He got off at 3 p.m. He is going to have to work this weekend. His new hours for this shift be Saturday and Sunday from 7 a.m.–7 p.m. And Monday and Tuesday from 3 p.m.–11 p.m. and off Wednesday, Thursday, and Friday.

Thursday, February 3, nothing happened today and it was really a nice day. I didn't have no kind of feeling at all of these awful wimps.

Friday, February 4, these imps were back again, not really bad though. They would just pick a little here and a little there.

Saturday, February 5, everything was okay, Al was at work, but George and his family were here with me.

Sunday, February 6, I thought everything was okay, but when me, George, and his wife and kids went to church. His son's stomach tore up real, real bad and we had to leave before Phillip even got a chance to preach anything. Sunday night, we didn't go to church, and little things started happening. Such as things that I have no problems dealing with, like maybe you would hear a noise that you could blame on something else or my ear would feel like something tickling it. And I would blame that on my hair, stuff like that.

Monday, February 7, at around 4 p.m. before anything started happening. George and Al had already left for work and no one was here except me and George's wife and kids. I can't even remember what happened first, but I do know that they really showed their butts. They would make the butter flip in the refrigerator. I would open the door to it and they picked at George's wife a lot, tickling her ears, rubbing her hair, or pulling her pant leg up. They would get behind my chair and pull back on the back of it like they were trying to flip the chair over in it. Sometimes they would tickle my ear or rub my hair. They even made my cross twirl with me wearing it! They would make my dream catcher and headdress twirl around, and if I would say something about oiling it, that would take them stop instantly.

IMPS, IMPS, AND MORE WIMPS!

I mean these things would be twirling real fast and then stop as quick as you could snap your finger. Dead still! They would nag us like this until Al and George came in from work at 12:45 a.m.

Tuesday, February 8, this was a real bad day! At first it wasn't that bad until Al and George went to work. Then it started up. Not real bad at first. Then I took my daughter home and Chris left at 5:30 p.m. going home that is when it really started. I had a picture of my house (which is in this book) and this figure looks like someone dressed up in a sheet. This friend of Juanita's said that it looked like to her that it was Jesus holding a cane. I couldn't see this, so I zoomed in on this thing. I shouldn't have done it because I saw this thing it I could see a face on it. It was a fat face, he had very little hair on top, and had a moustache and beard. I decided that I would darken it so I could see it better, but instead it came out like this following this page. It really shook me up pretty bad. I reached up to call another on my cordless phone and it had "Extension in use"; this comes up on my phone when someone has the phone up in another room. I checked their phones and no one had any of the receivers up. I unplugged every phone in the house, except my cordless phone and it still read "Extension in use." That upset me even more. I couldn't call out and no one could call in. I had a cellular phone too, so I used it and called my mother and told her what all was going on and had happened. So she called Phillip and told him what happened. I had a cellular phone too, so I used it and called mother and told her what all was going on and had happened. So she called Phillip and told him what had happened. She had misunderstood me, and she told Phillip that I was in my van and wouldn't go back in the house. Phillip said that upset him so he carne right over. When he got here, he acted like that it had made him mad and I sensed it very hard that he didn't really want to come. Now this part gets con using. He didn't want to be here so it made him mad, but when he left about an hour and a half after he gets here, he says, "If you need me, call me. And I'll be right back over here if you need me to."

While he was here, he looked at the picture I printed out and the original picture. He said between this and the way phone was doing, it really had him puzzled. We prayed and then he left. About five to ten minutes after he left, I made the remark that I wondered what the phone would do if I was to oil it, and as soon as I said that, my phone started back to working. A short while later, Al and George came in and we told them what had happened. A1 already knew because he called me right after I got to working again. After this, we went to bed.

Wednesday, February 9. Everything was okay to because Al was at home.

Thursday, February 10. At 1:15 a.m. the phone rung and woke me up. When I answered the phone, they hung up. I went to the bathroom and then came back to bed, and by the time my head hit the pillow, the phone rang again. They hung up again. So l went ahead and got up. I fixed a cup of instant coffee and drank it, made me another cup, then made a pot of coffee. While sitting here drinking coffee, I heard something that sound like someone taking their fingernails and running them down the grate on my air conditioner. The first thing that happened though was a piece of paper flipping over on the table. I could make up an excuse for that, then I heard that other in the hall of the finger nails. I kinda froze for a second or two and then I heard spoons clinging together at my sink, there were three spoons lying over on the counter. I didn't like that at all. So I downed my cup of coffee and went to bed. After I got in there, I told my husband what had happened and no sooner than I told him he was back asleep. As I lay there, my bed went to shaking again. I don't what it is but I do know for sure that there is something here. Phillip and Al was talking about this Wednesday at church bothered Phillip that Tuesday night when all of this stuff started up like it did. I know that it had made him mad and just him either. I feel that it made several of them mad that is in his family. I always thought that a preacher was supposed to be there to help you when you are in need of some answers, but I have learnt through experience that, that is just not true. I don't like the way people at that church shunned me away from them, when I am trying to talk to them. Al says that I need to mingle with them, but how can I when they shun me away? Al just doesn't see all this because he is always too busy talking to the women in there and Phillip and his wife and his daddy. If I say something about leaving the church, Al gets mad at me. So what am I supposed to do?

Friday, February 11. Nothing happened today, everything was okay.

Saturday, February 12. Today I will end my book. Before I do though, there are some things I need to say. Tuesday night after Al and George came home and we went to bed, I had a bad dream that woke me up, crying and asking Phillip not to let them things get me. I was hiding behind him. I don't know what all the dream says about, I just remember that part of the dream. And I also had the same dream Wednesday night as well. Friday night (which was last night) I had two dreams. One really weird. I am scared of things being twirled around, and I dreamed that George's wife found three yo-yo's and was going to throw them away. My daddy got them and started playing with them. I told him not to because they have always made me nervous and all he did is just laugh and started playing with them anyway. I spoke up and very nervous. The next dream I had was really good, but at the same time, it was weird. I dreamed Al and I was at some hospital and I had gotten lost. These two older men was walking the hall almost beside me and I had the feeling that they were following me for some reason. I turned to a hall that was a dead end and one of the old men followed me. I told him if he didn't leave me alone, I was going to douse him with this oil and I pulled it out of my pocket and when he saw it, he said, "We better leave her alone before because she is a Christian," and then both of them disappeared. I found myself outside and saw Al parking the van. Next thing I knew he and Phillip was coming to meet me to show me where the van was. All of a sudden, Al disappeared, and I found him in a parked car with Phillip's wife and family. I turned to look at Phillip and he was gone. I turned to look back at Al and he was getting out of Phillip's car. I found myself in the driver's side of my van, and I left Al with Phillip and his family and then my dream ended.

About the Author

Charlotte M. Prosser was born on July 21, 1954, in Opelika, Alabama. She has three children and has been married to her husband for thirty-one years and has ten grandchildren and two great-grandchildren. She attended Phillips Junior College about seventeen years ago but didn't graduate, even though she earned a 4.0 grade average. Because she didn't have a high school diploma, they wouldn't let her graduate college. She was going to church at the Living Word Assembly of God and had created a directory book for the church.

Mrs. Prosser wants everyone to know that all she wrote in her book is true and based on her own her own personal experience. She hopes every reader who buys and enjoys *Imps, Imps, and More Wimps!* Charlotte writes, "I have learnt to trust in God very strongly, but not as much as I want to."

www.ingramcontent.com/pod-product-compliance
Lightning Source LLC
LaVergne TN
LVHW040200080526
838202LV00042B/3256